War Horse

by Michael Morpurgo

Lit Link
Grades 7-8

Written by Ruth Solski
Illustrated by On The Mark Press

About the Author:
Ruth Solski was an educator for over 30 years. She has written many educational resources and is the founder of S&S Learning Materials. As a writer, her main goal is to provide teachers with a useful resource they can implement in their classrooms to bring the joy of learning to children. This Lit Link is dedicated to my daughter, Lisa Solski, who being an equestrian rider has a love and passion for horses.

On The Mark Press
15 Dairy Avenue
Napanee, Ontario
K7R 1M4
www.onthemarkpress.com

OTM-14287 ISBN: 9781770787995

1

At A Glance

Learning Expectations	Chapters 1 & 2	Chapters 3 & 4	Chapters 5 & 6	Chapters 7 & 8	Chapters 9 & 10	Chapters 11 & 12	Chapters 13 & 14	Chapters 15 & 16	Chapters 17 & 18	Chapters 19 & 20	Chapter 21
Reading Comprehension											
• Recalling events	•	•	•	•	•	•	•			•	•
• Noting details	•	•	•	•	•	•	•		•	•	•
• Classifying story events				•			•				
• Summarize events and story details			•								
• Identify and describe story events		•				•					
• Sequencing events in a story						•	•		•	•	
Reasoning and Critical Thinking Skills											
• Character traits, comparisons			•								
• Making inferences	•					•		•			
• Developing opinions			•			•			•		
• Finding proof		•								•	
Vocabulary Development, Grammar & Word Usage											
• Alphabetical order	•										
• Antonyms, synonyms, homophones	•	•					•	•	•		
• Root words, syllabication		•					•				
• Parts of speech		•		•	•					•	
• Word meanings			•								
• Compound words				•					•		
• Types of sentences									•		

Table of Contents

WAR HORSE

By Michael Morpurgo

Learning Expectations:

• To introduce students to the writings of Michael Morpurgo.
• To make students aware of the effects that World War I made on people, countries, and animals.
• To provide students with a reading experience in which the narrator is an animal.
• To provide practice in a wide variety of reading, writing, and grammar skills.
• To have students discover and interpret new vocabulary and colloquial expressions.

Story Summary:

War Horse

Joey is a six month old gangling colt who is sold at an auction to a drunken farmer who bought him to spite a neighbor he disliked. Fortunately for Joey, the farmer had a son who fell in love with him instantly and raises him with great love and care. Albert trains Joey to plow fields along with Zoey, another farm horse, successfully in order to help his father win a foolish bet he made when he was drunk.

War breaks out in Europe. Albert's father is desperate for money to pay his mortgage and sells Joey to the army. Joey is taken away from Albert to become a cavalry horse. While being trained for the cavalry Joey meets Topthorn, a beautiful black stallion, who will also be a cavalry horse. They become great friends and are seldom apart.

On the battlefield in France, the horses lead a cavalry charge into enemy machine gun fire and many soldiers are killed or wounded. German troops take Joey and Topthorn are taken to a farm where they meet Emilie, a young French girl, who cares for them. During their stay at the farm, the horses pulled a farm cart that carried injured men from the battlefield to the army hospital. Later Joey and Topthorn are taken from the farm and used to pull a heavy artillery gun. Sick and very exhausted Topthorn collapses and dies on the battlefield.

Joey is very distraught and runs off and ends up in "no man's land" which is an area that separates enemy lines. While wandering in the area looking for food, Joey is saved by two soldiers. A German soldier and a Welsh soldier realize Joey has a problem and flip a coin to see which side will help him. Joey is taken to a British veterinary hospital where he is reunited with Albert who is now a soldier in the British army.

Unfortunately Joey's life is still in danger as he has acquired tetanus from the barbed wire wound. Months of tender care by Albert and the other troopers and his will to live help him to

WAR HORSE

By Michael Morpurgo

survive this deadly disease. When the war finally comes to an end, Joey and Albert have another hurdle to jump. All the horses that are still alive after the war will not be returning home with the troops on the ships.

All the horses are to be auctioned off to local farmers and butchers. The troopers all contribute money to a collection made by Sergeant Thunder in an attempt to buy Joey for Albert. Unfortunately, a local butcher outbids Sergeant Thunder. It seems that Joey's future is doomed until Emilie's grandfather steps in and outbids the butcher.

Emilie's grandfather has kept the promise he made to her before she died. He has bought Joey and plans to take him home until he finds out how much Albert loves Joey. He then decides to sell Joey to Albert for a penny and makes him promise to love and care for Joey for the rest of his life.

Author Biography:

Michael Morpurgo

Michael Morpurgo was born on October 5, in 1943. He is a British author, poet, playwright, and librettist. He is best known for his work in children's literature.

Many of his relatives have been involved in various dramatic careers such as acting, music, and poetry writing. Michael was educated at a variety of schools in London, Devon, Sussex, and Kent. His unhappy experience at a boarding school resulted in one of his most famous works "*The Butterfly Lion.*" Later he attended London University to study English and French and then became a teacher in a primary school in Kent. It was here that he discovered what he wanted to do.

While teaching, he found out that children loved the stories that he told rather than the ones that he read to them. These stories were magical for his students and he realized there was magic in it for him. The part, of writing, Michael loves the most is making up the story while daydreaming. The hardest part is writing it down. He loves finishing it and holding the book in his hand while sharing the story with others.

In 1976, Michael and his wife Clare started a charity called "*Farms for City Children.*" This charity provides children living in city and urban areas the opportunity to spend a week working actively and purposely on a farm in the countryside. They now own three farms. For over thirty years 50,000 children from cities and towns throughout the UK have spent time at one.

WAR HORSE

By Michael Morpurgo

Teacher Information on World War I

World War I began in 1914. It involved may countries, killed many soldiers as well as citizens and caused a great deal of destruction to countries, cities, farmland, and historical buildings. It ended in 1918. World War I was started by an assasins bullet which killed the Archduke Francis Ferdinand of Austria-Hungary and his wife in Sarjevo, the capital of Austria-Hungary's province of Bosnia-Herzegovina. The assassin was Gavrilo Princip, a Serbian terrorist.

World War I was fought on land, sea, and in the air. Early airplanes, tanks, submarines, and machine guns were used. Many men fought in the trenches that zigzagged across the land. A trench was 6 to 8 feet (18 to 21 meters) deep and wide enough for two men to pass each other. Soldiers lived in dugouts for protection. Barbed wire was used to protect the trenches from enemy soldiers. Between the enemy trenches lay a stretch of ground called "no man's land."

Life in the trenches was miserable. The smell of dead bodies lingered in the air, rats searching for food ran everywhere, and soldiers had problems keeping clean and dry. Enemy artillery and machine guns kept each side pinned in the trenches. When the order came "Over the Top!", soldiers scrambled out of the trenches and dashed across no man's land with fixed bayonets on their guns. Grenades were hurled into the trenches and soldiers struggled to get through the barbed wire getting out. Many of the soldiers were killed by enemy machine guns. A deadly gas developed by the Germans was used during the war and its fumes caused vomiting and suffocation.

World War I caused terrible destruction in the Euopean countries involved. Nearly 10 million soldiers died as a result of the war. Thousands of horses died in the cavalry. Approximately 21 million men were wounded. Armies destroyed farms and villages as they passed through them. Factories, bridges, and railroad lines were destroyed. Land became barren by artillery shells, trenches, and chemicals. Many countries were left with enormous war debts.

Teacher Input Suggestions:

1. Read the novel and this lit link before beginning any class work.

2. With the assistance of the school resource teacher, select the other novels written by Michael Morpurgo and display them in the classroom at a reading center.

3. Review all the activities carefully. Select those which meets the needs of your students.

4. Do not expect students to complete all the activities. The activities can be modified or extended by selecting activities for individual students.

WAR HORSE
By Michael Morpurgo

5. The activities could also be completed by groups of students during discussions orally. Each group would have a leader who would ask the questions. The leader would also have the Answer Key to check for correct answers. Other concepts could also be duscussed at the same time such as emotions, suspense, events, characters, conditions, etc.

6. Duplicate the activity sheets as needed.

7. Duplicate the cover sheet found on page 13 for the students to use in their workbook or binder.

8. Display picture of different types of horses and photos of World War I soldiers, machinery, vehicles, trenches, and military battles.

9. Show the movies of War Horse and Paschendale to your class.

10. Have the students compare the movie of War Horse to the story in the novel. Have them note the similarities and differences. Discuss the changes made by the movie director and why the students think they were made.

11. Discuss the facts that the students learned about World War I from reading the book and watching the movie.

12. Discuss the facts the students gained about horses from the novel.

13. Display a labelled diagram of a horse in the classroom for the students to refer to during the reading of the novel.

14. During an art lesson have the students illustrate their favorite scene in the novel for a display.

15. Discuss why the usage of horses in World War I was a military move that turned out to be a tragedy.

16. Discuss the pros and cons of a war on a chart.

17. Bring in a guest speaker who can discuss horses and their usage in the past and the present.

18. Invite a historian who is quite knowledgeable about World War I to answer questions that students may have about the war.

WAR HORSE
By Michael Morpurgo

Glossary of Words

Chapter One:

- **barney**: British slang for a quarrel, disturbance, row
- **bellowed**: a loud deep noise; roar; to shout in a loud deep voice
- **confusion**: disorder; mistaking one thing for another
- **consolation**: to console; comfort a person or thing
- **conviction**: certainty; assurance; belief
- **divil**: British slang for devil
- **draught horse**: a horse used for pulling heavy loads
- **firebrand**: agitator; someone who arouses angry feelings
- **gangling**: akwardly tall and slender; lank and loosely built
- **guineas**: old English coins no longer used.
- **haggling**: to bargain over a price or the terms of a bargain
- **halter**: a rope or strap with a rope used for leading animals
- **hubbub**: a loud confused noise; uproar
- **instinctive**: using one's natural feelings; not learned
- **lunge**: to move suddenly forward
- **nickered**: to neigh
- **obstinate**: not giving in; stubborn
- **parish**: a district that has its own church and clergyman; a community
- **recoiled**: draw back; shrink back; flinch
- **stamina**: strength; endurance; power to resist
- **suckle**: to find milk from the breast or udder; nurse
- **thoroughbred**: any one of a breed of horses used for racing or jumping
- **twick**: old English for tweak which is a sudden jerk or pull
- **vicious**: evil; wicked; spiteful; fierce; bad disposition
- **violently**: fiercely; forcefully; very strong feelings
- **wrenched**: to pull or twist violently

Chapter Two:

- **abundance**: great plenty; full supply
- **companion**: friend; comrade
- **devilish**: like the devil; very cruel; wicked
- **encounter**: to meet unexpectedly
- **gawkishness**: cluminess; awkwardness
- **hesitated**: undecided; held back
- **infinite**: without limits or bounds; endless
- **intricacies**: many twists and turns; complicated
- **molly-coddled**: to make a fuss over; pampered
- **obedience**: doing what one is told to do
- **precaution**: care taken beforehand
- **pretext**: false reason concealing the real reason
- **prowess**: bravery; daring; courage; valor
- **resolution**: a thing decided on; a decision made
- **vengeance**: revenge; punishment for a wrong
- **whinnied**: soft or gentle quavering sound a horse makes

Chapter Three:

- **acute**: sharp and severe
- **acknowledged**: admitted to be true or to exist
- **arbitrating**: giving a decision in a dispute
- **bullocks**: oxen; steers
- **conceded**: admitted it is true; acknowledged
- **copse**: a thicket of small trees, bushes or shrubs
- **foreboding**: a prediction; warning; omen
- **inevitable**: sure to happen; could not be avoided
- **inquisitiveness**: asking many questions; curiosity
- **normality**: normal conditions; usual happening
- **negotiator**: a person who helps solve problems
- **pique**: feeling anger at being slighted; wounded pride
- **reassure**: to restore confidence
- **suspicious**: questionable; doubtful
- **tension**: mental or nervous strain
- **vehemently**: having or showing strong feelings; eager; passionate

Chapter Four:

- **apprehension**: expectation of misfortune; fear; dread
- **artillery**: mounted guns manned by a crew
- **cavalry**: soldiers who fight on horseback

WAR HORSE

By Michael Morpurgo

- **console**: soothe; cheer up; comfort
- **fetlock**: the tuft of hair above a horse's hoof on the back part of the leg
- **jodhpurs**: breeches or pants for horseback riding
- **khaki**: a dull yellowish-brown color
- **military**: the army; soldiers, officers
- **recruiting**: to get men and women to join the armed forces
- **regiment**: a unit of an army made up of several battalions or squadrons of soldiers organized in one large group usually commanded by a colonel
- **regulations**: rules or laws used to control a system
- **specimen**: one of a group or class
- **yeomanry**: a British volunteer cavalry force organised for internal defense in 1907

Chapter Five:
- **barracks**: a building or group of buildings for soldiers to live in
- **canter**: a gentle gallop
- **charge**: attack; to rush to with force
- **cumbersome**: hard to manage; clumsy; unwielding
- **defeatist**: a person who expects, wishes for , or expects defeat
- **devotion**: deep steady affection; loyalty; faithfulness
- **echelon**: a unit of an army such as a company, battalion, division or corps
- **gallop**: the fastest gait of a horse; all feet are off the ground together in one stride
- **infantry**: soldiers trained, equipped, and organized to fight on foot
- **infuriated**: to fill with wild fierce anger; furious
- **imperceptibly**: very slight; gradual; subtle or indistinct
- **manoeuvres**: (British) planned movement of troops
- **mess**: the place where soldiers take meals
- **revelled**: to take very great pleasure in; enjoy immensely
- **rubbish**: silly words; nonsense
- **sabres**: (British) a heavy sword used by the cavalry
- **squadron**: military unit made up of 120 to 200 soldiers led by a major or a colonel

- **tedious**: long and tiresome; wearisome
- **transformation**: a change in appearance
- **trepidation**: nervous; dread; fear; fright
- **troopers**: soldiers in the cavalry with the rank of private
- **trot**: to go at a gait between a walk and a run
- **unerring**: free of error; exactly right

Chapter Six:
- **barrage**: a barrier of artillery fire to check the enemy or to protect one's own soldiers in advancing or retreating
- **bivouacked**: encampment; place where soldiers camp for a period of time
- **buoyant**: able to float
- **column**: an arrangement of soldiers in short rows one behind another used for marching
- **composure**: calmness; quietness; self-control
- **dug-outs**: trenches used for soldiers for protection
- **expectancy**: looking forward to; hoped for
- **expeditionary**: a group of soldiers sent to help
- **exurberance**: joyfulness; happiness
- **flank**: the far right or the far side of an army, fleet or military formation
- **greatcoat**: a heavy overcoat worn by soldiers
- **obliterate**: destroy; wipe out; erase
- **optimism**: to look on the bright side
- **peremptory**: leaving no choice; final; absolute
- **quay-side**: a solid landing place for ships
- **reveille**: a signal on a bugle or a whistle or a drum to waken soldiers in the morning
- **sentries**: soldiers who stand at a post to watch and guard against surprises
- **tethered**: tied to a stake with a rope or chain
- **trenches**: long narrow ditches dug by soldiers for protection during a war

Chapter Seven:
- **apprentice**: a person learning a trade
- **ammunition**: bullets; shells; gunpowder; shot; bombs
- **bandoliers**: belts worn over the shoulders across the chest used to carry bullets, gunpowder or fuses
- **barbed wire**: wire with sharp points to keep people or animals in

WAR HORSE

By Michael Morpurgo

- **battlefield**: the place where a battle is fought
- **bayonet**: a blade used for piercing or stabbing attached to the muzzle of a gun
- **bleakest**: depressing; cheerless; dismal
- **chafings**: to become sore by rubbing
- **deadlock**: a condition or time when two opponents are equally strong and will not give in
- **finesse**: skillful handling of a difficult situation
- **forelock**: a lock of hair that hangs down over the forehead of a horse
- **grumbler**: a person who always complains
- **haggard**: looking worn from pain, tiredness, worry or hunger
- **haversack**: a bag or pouch used by soldiers for carrying food, utensils while on a march
- **incessantly**: without stopping; all the time
- **inseparable**: always together; can't be apart
- **meticulous**: extremely careful of small details
- **monotony**: lack of variety; boring
- **ominous**: of bad omen; unfavorable; threathening
- **resilence:** the power of springing back
- **respiratory:** having something to do with breathing or used for breathing
- **skirmishes**: brief fights between small groups
- **unsympathetic**: without sympathy; don't feel sorry for
- **windgall**: a soft tumor or swelling at the fetlock on a horse's leg

Chapter Eight:
- **bedlam**: noisy confusion; uproar
- **carnage**: the slaughter of a great number of people; massacre
- **crump**: to crunch; a large explosive shell (British slang)
- **farewells**: good-byes; wishes of good luck
- **foe**: enemy; anything that harms or is likely to injure
- **ghastly**: horrible; frightful; shocking
- **inexorably**: unrelenting; immovable; implacable
- **strewn**: scattered; sprinkled

Chapter Nine:
- **bristled**: to stand up straight; to show one is ready and willing to fight
- **clogs**: wooden shoes
- **compensate**: pay; to make amends

- **corpses**: dead bodies of human beings; remains
- **dishevelled**: not neat; rumpled; messy; untidy
- **exhaustion**: extreme fatigue from great exertion
- **fodder**: coarse food for horses, cattle and other domestic animals
- **gait**: the kind of steps in going along
- **intimidated**: made afraid; frightened
- **lavished**: given freely; extravagant
- **sacrilege**: an intentional injury to anything sacred or held sacred; disrespectful

Chapter Ten:
- **adulation:** highest level of love and admiration
- **campaigners**: to take part in a campaign
- **devastating**: causing widespread destruction; deflating
- **extricate**: to set free; release
- **hazardous**: dangerous; risky
- **misery**: miserable; unhappy state of mind
- **momentum**: impulse; force

Chapter Eleven:
- **beseiged:** to try for a long time to take by force
- **bespectacled**: wearing glasses
- **emerged**: came out; came into view
- **exuberant**: abounding with good health and bright spirits
- **incessant**: never stopping; continual
- **lorries**: British motor trucks; a long flat horse-drawn wagon
- **scythe**: a long slightly curved blade on a long handle used for cutting hay or long grasses
- **transition**: a change of passing from one condition, place, thing or activity
- **urgency**: being urgent; need for immediate attention

Chapter Twelve:
- **appalling:** to fill with horror or fear; dismay; terrify
- **arduous**: hard to do; strenuous; requiring much effort
- **compulsion**: use of force; an impulse that is hard to resist

OTM-14287 ISBN: 9781770787995

WAR HORSE

By Michael Morpurgo

- **deteriorated**: made worse; lessen in character, quality, and value
- **diminutive**: small, little, tiny
- **excruciatingly**: very painful; torturing; extreme pain
- **exposure**: laying open; exposing; disclose; unmask
- **flaxen**: pale-yellow in color
- **idyllic**: simple and charming; rustic
- **interminable**: never stopping; unceasing; endless
- **meagre**: poor or scanty; thin or lean
- **muster**: to gather together; to collect; to assemble
- **piteous**: to be pitied; to move one's heart
- **ponderously**: heavy and clumsy; unweilding; cumbersome
- **priority**: importance; preference
- **ration**: a fixed amount of food; daily allowance of food
- **recuperation**: recovery from a sickness
- **shrapnel**: an artillery shell filled with pellets and powder
- **spasmodically**: jerkily; choppily; suddenly and violently
- **stench**: a very bad smell; foul odor; stink

Chapter Thirteen:
- **benighted**: not knowing right from wrong; ignorant
- **chortling**: chuckle or snort with glee
- **empathy**: understands and imagines others feelings and emotions
- **protestations**: protest; disapprovel
- **strenuous:** vigorous; requiring much energy

Chapter Fourteen:
- **abomination**: anything that arouses strong disgust or hate
- **divinity**: a devine being; divine nature or quality

- **inclination**: tendency; preference; leaning, bending
- **intensified**: strengthened; increased
- **midday**: middle of the day
- **nobility**: people of noble rank, title or birth
- **personify**: to be a type of; exemplify
- **regal**: fit for a king
- **serenity**: quietness; peacefulness; calmness
- **vigorously**: full of vigor; strong and active in body and mind

Chapter Fifteen:
- **belched**: thrown out with force
- **bombardment**: an attack with heavy fire with large guns
- **brigadier**: an officer in command of a brigade
- **compelled**: to bring about by force; commanded
- **corridor**: a hallway; a narrow strip of land connecting two countries
- **inexorably**: unrelentlng; implacable; unyielding
- **intermittent**: stopping and starting; pausing at intervals
- **overwhelmed**: to overcome completely; crush
- **shelling**: to fire cannon or mortar shells

Chapter Sixteen:
- **askew**: turned or twisted; out of proper position
- **consternation**: great dismay; paralysing terror
- **impenetrable**: cannot be entered, pierced or passed
- **interspersed**: scattered among other things
- **jinking**: to elude by dodging; to make a quick turn
- **methodically**: in the same speed and manner
- **reconciliation**: bringing together again in friendship
- **savour**: a taste or smell; flavor; to enjoy
- **subsided**: to die down; become less active
- **vantage**: a better condition or position
- **wafting**: waving; blowing gently

Chapters Seventeen and Eighteen:
- **cauterized:** to burn with a hot iron; used to prevent wounds from bleeding
- **euphoric**: feeling of happiness and bodily well-being
- **incredulous**: not ready to believe; doubting
- **immaculate**: without a spot or stain; very neat and clean

OTM-14287 ISBN: 9781770787995

WAR HORSE

By Michael Morpurgo

- **irrational**: unreasonable; unable to think and reason clearly
- **kinship**: family relationship; resemblance
- **tetanus**: a disease that enters the body through a cut or wound; it may cause death
- **tremor**: quaking, quivering, shaking of the body
- **zealously**: eagerly, earnestly, enthusiastically

Chapters Nineteen, Twenty, and Twenty-One

- **brooding**: hovering closely around; dwelling moodily upon a thought
- **casualties**: members of the armed services who have been killed, wounded or captured
- **commiserating**: to feel or express sorrow for another's suffering
- **conspiracy**: secret planning to do something wrong
- **convalescence**: gradual recovery of health and strength after an illness
- **dimish**: to make smaller in size or amount
- **dispersed**: scatter; to send or drive off in different directions
- **glistened**: to shine, sparkled
- **inconsolable**: broken-hearted; not to be comforted
- **jauntily**: easy; carefree; lively
- **levity**: lightness of mind; not serious; flippant
- **pasties**: English meat pies
- **profound**: very deep; felt deeply; very great
- **rapturous**: full of feeling; estactic; blissful
- **skittish**: easily frightened; apt to jump, run or start
- **tandem**: one behind the other
- **unswerving**: unwavering; firm
- **vagaries**: fads; extravagent notions

Old English Expressions/Meanings

- **brook no refusal**: will not tolerate the answer no
- **such a hiding**: such a beating, thrashing
- **'cos I didn't want to put you off**: because I didn't want to make you upset
- **lightings up**: small sticks used to start a fire
- **whilst**: while
- **s'pose**: suppose
- **beast of burden**: an animal used to pull heavy loads
- **smithy**: blacksmith
- **p'raps**: perhaps
- **can't 'ardly**: can't hardly
- **'cept**: except
- **'im**: him
- **'is**: his
- **'as**: has
- **'cos**: because
- **'cepting**: excepting
- **savin'**: saving
- **e'd**: he'd
- **'ave**: have
- **layabouts**: idle persons, lazy, loafers
- **'ullabaloo**: hullabaloo - an uproar
- **'opes**: hopes
- **'ole**: whole
- **'ammer**: hammer
- **'appen**: happen
- **'elp**: help
- **shut eye**: sleep, rest
- **you are Tommy**: slang for you are a British soldier

WAR HORSE

By Michael Morpurgo

Name: _____

OTM-14287 ISBN: 9781770787995 13

WAR HORSE
By Michael Morpurgo

Author's Note

1. How does the author introduce the main character in the novel.

_____

_____

2. Describe the horse's appearance.

_____

_____

_____

3. What is the name of the horse and who painted his portrait?

_____

_____

4. When was the portrait painted?

_____

_____

5. What terrible event had begun in the same year as the painting?

_____

_____

6. Why do only a few people in the village remember Joey?

_____

_____

7. Why did the author write this story about Joey?

_____

_____

8. List things that you know about World War I.

_____

_____

_____

_____

_____

_____

_____

WAR HORSE

By Michael Morpurgo

Chapter One

A. Answer the questions with sentences.

1. Who is narrating the story?

_____

_____

2. Describe the young horse's appearance.

_____

_____

3. Why was the horse sale a terrifying event for the young horse?

_____

_____

4. Why was the young horse difficult to sell?

_____

_____

_____

5. Who bought the horse? Tell why.

_____

_____

_____

6. What was Albert's father suppose to buy at the market?

_____

_____

7. Why will Albert's father never be the young horse's master?

_____

_____

8. How did the young horse suffer on his trip to the owner's farm?

_____

_____

WAR HORSE
By Michael Morpurgo

Chapter One

9. How do you know horses are able to communicate with one another?

_____

_____

10. Describe how Albert befriended the young horse.

_____

_____

_____

11. What did Albert name the young horse and why?

_____

_____

12. What problems may Albert have with his father?

_____

_____

B. Word Study: Record each group of words in alphabetical order.

1. gangling, glimpse, gritted, gently, groom

_____

2. hubbub, harsh, halter, hauled, huddled

_____

3. strength, stamina, screamed, stranded, struggle

_____

4. thoroughbred, thirteen, through, tailboard, touch

_____

5. lunge, lone, lacked, life, leant

_____

6. exhaustion, excited, echoing, eating, enough

_____

7. memories, master, market, mane, managed

_____

8. bucket, bidding, barney, brought, beaming

_____

WAR HORSE

By Michael Morpurgo

Chapter Two

A. Answer the questions with sentences.

1. What did Albert do with his free time on the farm?

_____

_____

2. How did Joey like his life on the farm?

_____

_____

_____

3. How did Joey feel about Albert's father?

_____

_____

4. Who was Joey's surprise visitor one Tuesday evening and why was he there?

_____

_____

_____

5. How did Joey react to Albert's father's raised stick?

_____

_____

_____

6. Why did Albert and his father come to the stables together the next morning?

_____

_____

_____

7. What might have happened to Joey if Albert's mother hadn't intervened?

_____

_____

WAR HORSE

By Michael Morpurgo

Chapter Two

8. What will happen to Joey if he isn't trained and if Albert's father loses his bet?

_____

_____

9. How did Albert's approach to training change Joey?

_____

_____

10. How do you know Albert sucessfuly trained Joey?

_____

_____

11. What was the important news Albert's father heard in the village?

_____

_____

12. How did Albert's parents react to the news?

_____

_____

_____

B. Record the words in the word box beside their synonyms.

companion	imitated	encounter	prowess
molly-coddled	recesses	cruel	survive
affection	bearable	pretext	precaution

1. reason _____

2. love _____

3. tolerate _____

4. corners _____

5. friend _____

6. safeguard _____

7. meeting _____

8. ability _____

9. spoiled _____

10. mean _____

11. live _____

12. reproduced _____

Chapter Three

A. Complete each sentence.

1. Albert's father no longer dealt with Joey and Zoey because _____

_____

2. There was a growing tension on the farm because_____

_____

3. Albert's mother told him he shouldn't blame his father because _____

_____

4. Albert's father drinks because_____

_____

5. Albert was angry with his mother because _____

_____

6. Albert's father feels they only need one horse on the farm because_____

_____

7. Albert's mother had to arbitrate between Albert and his father because _____

_____

8. Albert agreed to return the Saddleback boar because _____

_____

9. Joey was not upset when Albert's father came in the stable the first time because _____

_____

Chapter Three

10. Joey was suspicious when Albert's father came the second time because _____

_____

_____

11. Albert's father had tricked Joey because _____

_____

_____

12. Albert's father feels badly about what is going to happen to Joey because _____

_____

_____

B. Beside each word record its root word on the line provided.

1. reasonable   _____   7. worries   _____

2. complaining   _____   8. piggery   _____

3. declared   _____   9. tightened   _____

4. hardly   _____   10. unusually   _____

5. ditches   _____   11. arbitrating   _____

6. angrily   _____   12. exchanges   _____

C. Match the words in the word box to their synonyms.

inquisitiveness	tension	foreboding	acute
vehemently	suspicious	arbitrator	copse
arbitrating	reasonable		

1. curiosity   _____   6. passionately   _____

2. uneasiness   _____   7. woodlot   _____

3. prediction   _____   8. questionable   _____

4. sharp   _____   9. settling   _____

5. problem-solver   _____   10. sensible   _____

Chapter Four

A. Locate a sentence in the chapter that proves each of the following statements is true. Record the first **five** words of the sentence and its **page number** on the line provided.

1. Albert's father was feeling guilty about what he was going to do.

_____

2. Joey was feeling nervous as they went into the village.

_____

3. Albert's father plans on selling Joey to the army.

_____

4. Captain Nicholls thought Albert's father was lying about the quality of the horse that he wanted to sell.

_____

5. Captain Nicholls would like to have Joey for his horse in the cavalry.

_____

6. Albert's father had previously agreed to sell Joey the day before.

_____

7. Captain Nicholls agrees to pay the price of forty pounds with one condition.

_____

8. Albert's father is afraid of being caught selling Joey.

_____

9. Joey passes the vet's examination.

_____

WAR HORSE
By Michael Morpurgo

Chapter Four

10. Albert's father feels very badly about selling Joey.

_____

11. Albert makes a promise to Joey.

_____

12. Captain Nicholls makes a commitment to Albert.

_____

B. Record the name of each underlined part of speech on the line provided.

1. <u>hushed</u> voice   _____

2. mounted Joey <u>swiftly</u>   _____

3. khaki <u>uniforms</u>   _____

4. Albert's father <u>dismounted</u>   _____

5. he <u>smoothed</u> my neck   _____

6. <u>fine</u> <u>young</u> horse   _____

7. he looked like a <u>shrunken</u> man   _____

8. stroked my <u>ears</u> gently   _____

C. Match the words in the box to their antonyms.

quietly	slowly	short	deep	finest
gently	opening	straight	buying	whispered

1. long   _____   6. shallow   _____

2. loudly   _____   7. crooked   _____

3. swiftly   _____   8. closing   _____

4. roughly   _____   9. shouted   _____

5. worst   _____   10. selling   _____

WAR HORSE

By Michael Morpurgo

Chapter Five

A. 1. Compare Joey's life as a farmhorse with his life as a cavalry horse. Complete the chart below.

Life as a Farmhorse	Life as a Cavalry Horse

2. Who visited Joey during his days of training? Tell why

_____

_____

3. Who is Captain Nicholls sending the painting to? Tell Why?

_____

_____

_____

4. How does Captain Nicholls feel about the war?

_____

_____

_____

WAR HORSE
By Michael Morpurgo

Chapter Five

5. Why does Captain Nicholls discuss Joey's training and care with Corporal Perkins?

_____

_____

_____

6. Did Corporal Perkins change his training methods? Tell how.

_____

_____

_____

7. How did Joey feel during the practice manoeuvres?

_____

_____

8. Who did Joey meet during the manoeuvres?

_____

_____

9. What event took place the next day?

_____

_____

B. Match each word in the word box to its meaning.

rubbish	trepidation	transformation	sabre
charge	tedious	devotion	revelled

1. deep feelings, loyalty, faithfulness _____

2. to enjoy immensely _____

3. a heavy sword used by the cavalry _____

4. nervous, dread, fear, fright _____

5. silly words, nonsense _____

6. long and tiring; wearisome _____

7. to rush at with force _____

8. a change in appearance _____

Chapter Six

A. Complete the following activities.

1. In point form describe the trip and the atmosphere on the liner to France.

   * _____
   * _____
   * _____
   * _____
   * _____
   * _____

2. Why did the mood of the troops and the horses change once they were docked and leaving the ship.

   _____
   _____

3. What did the troops realize when they saw the wounded men everywhere?

   _____
   _____

4. List the ways the horses received care during the march.

   * _____
   * _____
   * _____
   * _____

5. How did Joey know they were getting closer to the fighting?

   _____
   _____
   _____

6. Who gave Joey support during the march?

   _____
   _____

WAR HORSE
By Michael Morpurgo

Chapter Six

7. What happened to Joey during the charge?

_____

_____

8. Why do you think Joey kept on running without Captain Nicholls?

_____

_____

9. Who stopped Joey from running away from the battle scene?

_____

_____

10. What did Captain Stewart tell Joey on the ride back to the troops?

_____

_____

11. At the end of the day how did Joey feel?

_____

_____

B. Explain these groups of words in a different way. You may have to use the dictionary.

1. shroud of despondency: _____

_____

2. an air of exuberance and expectancy: _____

_____

3. buoyant with optimism: _____

_____

4. overwrought and apprehensive: _____

_____

5. mounts were tethered: _____

_____

6. growling crescendo of the big guns: _____

_____

7. sap my strength: _____

_____

WAR HORSE

By Michael Morpurgo

Chapter Seven

A. Number the events that took place in the chapter in the correct order.

_____ During a few minor skirmishes the troopers would dismount and leave their horses behind in the care of other riders.

_____ Topthorn and Joey spent the winter keeping each other sheltered from the snow and sleet and watched the cheery troopers go to the front line and those who returned haggard and silent.

_____ Trooper Warren tells Joey that he has given him back his confidence to ride a horse again.

_____ The battlefield was a wilderness filled with trenches crammed with men, shellholes, and barbed wire.

_____ Captain Stewart introduces Trooper Warren to Joey and tells Joey to take care of him.

_____ Eventually Trooper Warren began to talk to Joey and told him all about his family and his life back home.

_____ Suddenly the guns stopped firing overhead, silence filled the air, the bugle was sounded, and Trooper Warren dug with his spurs and said "Do me proud Joey."

_____ Joey and Topthorn no longer walked side by side because Joey was ridden by a trooper and they followed the officers.

_____ Joey enjoyed Trooper Warren's wonderful care but all he wished for was someone else to ride him.

_____ Joey realizes very quickly that Trooper Warren is not a good horseman.

_____ During the winter the cavalry could not participate in the fighting because the ground was not hard enough.

_____ One cold night in spring, the troopers saddled their horses, packed their gear, and moved silently out of camp onto a road and headed for the battlefield.

Chapter Seven

B. In the box below, illustrate the part of this chapter that you liked the best.

C. Skim through the chapter to find compound words that have the following meanings.

1. a person who rides a horse _____

2. someone who shoes horses _____

3. groups of horses used during the war _____

4. to begin or start _____

5. invade; to run over; crush _____

6. to come to a complete standstill _____

7. a shelter in the ground used during the war _____

8. side by side; at the side of _____

9. used to feed a horse _____

10. a heavy coat worn by a trooper _____

11. hair that hangs over a horse's forehead _____

12. a type of vehicle used in the war _____

WAR HORSE

By Michael Morpurgo

Chapter Eight

A. Classify the statements below as "True" or "False" on the lines provided.

_____ 1. The troopers began shooting at the enemy as soon as they entered no man's land.

_____ 2. Trooper Warren was very upset when he saw there was still wire on the battlefield.

_____ 3. The squadron continued riding forward despite the shells falling, the men crying out, and horses screaming out in fear and pain.

_____ 4. The troopers could not get close to the trenches because there were no holes blasted through the wire.

_____ 5. The enemy in the trenches shot at the troopers in the cavalry as they approached.

_____ 6. The troopers were being killed by shots coming from higher up amongst groups of trees.

_____ 7. Fortunately none of the horses were trapped in the barbed wire.

_____ 8. The only way through was to jump over the barbed wire.

_____ 9. Captain Stewart and Trooper Warren were captured by enemy soldiers.

_____ 10. The horses, Captain Stewart and Trooper Warren were all prisoners of war.

Chapter Eight

B. List the sounds heard on the battlefield that were mentioned in the chapter.

_____

_____

_____

_____

C. What did Captain Stewart hoped the people in charge would now understand?

_____

_____

D. Name the part(s) of speech underlined in each sentence.

1. We picked our <u>way</u> around the <u>craters</u> keeping our <u>line</u> as best we could. _____

2. The troopers were <u>shouting</u> at an invisible foe, <u>leaning</u> over their horses' necks, their

   sabres <u>stretched</u> out in front of them. _____

3. The riders tried <u>feverishly</u> to extract their horses from the wire. _____

4. The <u>riderless</u> horses galloped back towards the <u>British</u> trenches. _____

5. We were escorted <u>over the brow</u> of a hill and <u>down into a village</u>. _____

6. Some of the horses ran into the wire <u>before they could be stopped</u>. _____

Chapter Nine

A. Number the events in the order that they took place in the chapter

_____ The officer ordered that the horses were to be unsaddled, rubbed down, fed, and watered.

_____ During the evening the horses had a surprise visit from a little girl and her grandfather.

_____ As he walked towards the horses the soldiers sprang back and quickly stood at attention.

_____ Joey and Topthorn were taken by two nervous soldiers to a hospital tent many miles from where they were captured.

_____ The doctor informs Herr Hauptmann that the horses are to be used for ambulance transport.

_____ All afternoon and evening Joey and Topthorn walked up to the lines, were loaded with injured men and brought them back to the field hospital.

_____ For the first time, since the war had started, Joey and Topthorn were kept in a stable and fed sweet hay and were given buckets of cool water.

_____ Soldiers surrounded the horses patting and stroking them.

_____ In no time Topthorn and Joey were lavished with clumsy kindness as the men had never handled horses before.

_____ Out of a tent emerged a tall officer in a long grey coat with a bandage around his head and a heavily bandaged foot

_____ At the end of the day the doctor told the orderlies to give Joey and Topthorn the best of care as they had saved many lives that day.

WAR HORSE

By Michael Morpurgo

Chapter Nine

B. What informaton does each group of words give you in the chapter.

Is it **who**, **what**, **why**, **when**, **where** or **how**?

1. in my turn _____
2. of wounded soldiers _____
3. down farm tracks _____
4. in a long grey coat _____
5. at present _____
6. in all directions _____
7. to prove a point _____
8. with red piping _____
9. with two orderlies _____
10. two nervous soldiers _____
11. with impatience _____
12. in all directions _____

13. through orchards _____
14. clumsy kindness _____
15. a long battle _____
16. in the trenches _____
17. before the war _____
18. the thunder of guns _____
19. all that afternoon _____
20. behind the light _____
21. back of the shed _____
22. almost night _____
23. a flickering light _____
24. along the roads _____

C. Record the name of each part of speech that is underlined on the line provided.

1. There was <u>blood</u> on his <u>coat</u>. _____

2. The horses were lavished with <u>clumsy</u> kindness. _____

3. I began to whisk my tail <u>with impatience</u>. _____

4. The officer was an <u>immensely</u> <u>tall</u> man. _____

5. The officer <u>mounted</u> the cart and <u>took</u> the reins. _____

6. The officer stroked our noses <u>tenderly</u>. _____

Chapter Ten

A. Complete the following activities:

1. List the ways the soldiers showed their respect for Joey and Topthorn.

_____

_____

_____

_____

2. Despite all of the praise and rewards from the soldiers, what memories have stayed the longest in Joey's mind?

_____

_____

_____

_____

3. Why are horses not afraid of children?

_____

_____

4. List the ways Emilie showed her love for Joey and Topthorn.

_____

_____

_____

5. What was different at the stable one early winter evening?

_____

_____

_____

6. How did the horses feel?

_____

_____

WAR HORSE

By Michael Morpurgo

Chapter Ten

7. What did Emilie's grandfather tell the horses when he returned with buckets of hot mash?

_____

_____

8. What does Emilie's grandfather fear?

_____

_____

9. What does Emilie's grandfather ask of the horses?

_____

_____

10. What made it difficult for the horses to pull the empty cart during the winter?

_____

_____

11. Why did the shelling and the flares lighting up the sky stop one night?

_____

_____

12. What good news did the horses hear upon their return to the stable that night

_____

_____

13. What was Emilie's bargain with the German doctor?

_____

_____

14. What did Emilie's grandfather mean when he said, "We've all had a Christmas present today?

_____

_____

WAR HORSE

By Michael Morpurgo

Chapter Eleven

A. Complete each beginning with a **good** ending that tells why it happened.

1. Joey and Topthorn were put out to graze in the meadow because _____

_____

2. Emilie could not get on Topthorn without help because _____

_____

3. A convoy of lorries stopped at the farm one day because_____

_____

4. Emilie's grandfather told her they had to live as they had always lived because

_____

5. The second group of soldiers were not like the gentle orderlies because_____

_____

6. One old soldier was friendly because _____

_____

7. The new horses in the field did not answer Joey's and Topthorn's calls because

_____

8. Emilie's grandfather did not trust the officer because _____

_____

9. Emilie's grandfather had no choice but to let the horses be taken because

_____

_____

10. Emilie was not to cry because_____

_____

Chapter Eleven

B. Skim through the chapter to locate the antonyms for the following words.

1. lightning   _____
2. more   _____
3. light   _____
4. roughly   _____
5. easily   _____
6. happy   _____

`7. short   _____
8. easy   _____
9. hard   _____
10. cry   _____
11. late   _____
12. after   _____

C. Complete each sentence with the correct homophone.

1. The horses felt _____ after their long journey. (week, weak)

2. Joey _____ the thundering hooves of the horses. (heard, herd)

3. It will be _____ when the war is over. (grate, great)

4. The _____ of horses pulled hard to get the cart out of the mud. (teem, team)

5. Everyone hoped that _____ would soon come. (peace, piece)

6. Emilie brushed Joey's _____ until it was smooth and shiny. (main, mane)

7. Albert gently held Joey's _____. (rains, reigns, reins)

8. Mother will _____ the apples for the pie. (pair, pear, pare)

D. Some words can be used as a noun and as a verb. Use each pair of words in sentences to show how they are used as a noun and as a verb

1. mash (verb): _____

2. mash (noun): _____

3. load (verb): _____

4. load (noun): _____

5. groom (verb): _____

6. groom (noun); _____

WAR HORSE

By Michael Morpurgo

Chapter Twelve

A. Complete the following activities.

1. List the ways that Joey noticed the war had become more devastating.

_____

_____

_____

_____

_____

2. Describe the working conditions that the teams of horses endured while pulling the big guns.

_____

_____

_____

_____

_____

3. The gun team was made up of six horses. Name the horse(s) that each sentence is describing.

> **Joey   Topthorn   Heinie   Coco   two golden Halflingers**

a) This pair of horses led the gun team. _____

b) I was placed behind Topthorn and beside Coco. _____

c) This horse was thin, little, and wiry. _____

d) We walked at the end of the team behind Joey and Coco. _____

Chapter Twelve

e) The soldiers laughed at the white patch-marks on my face. _____

f) He was the only one on the team that had height and strength to pull as a gun horse.

   _____

g) This horse had the nastiest temper and often bit and kicked while he was eating.

   _____

h) This pair on the team were small, dun-colored ponies with flaxen manes and tails

   _____

i) The largest horse on the team was the first to lose weight and looked like a skinny creature.

   _____

j) This horse was moved beside Topthorn to replace Heinie. _____

k) A flying piece of shrapnel hit this horse in the neck and killed him. _____

l) This team member was failing in strength, in pain, and had a terrible cough.

   _____

m) This horse was lead away and shot after the vet's inspection. _____

n) He was worried about Topthorn and kept nuzzling him and licking him to keep him warm.

   _____

B. Record on the line provided the number of syllables in each of the following words.

   1. ponderously _____   2. muster _____   3. intermittently _____

   4. nuzzling _____   5. stride _____   6. deteriorated _____

   7. stench _____   8. meagre _____   9. spasmodically _____

   10. ration _____   11. intermidable   12. ambulance _____

   13. incongruous _____   14. priority _____   15. exposure _____

WAR HORSE
By Michael Morpurgo

Chapter Thirteen

A. Answer the following questions with sentences.

1. What did spring bring to Topthorn and Joey?

_____

_____

_____

_____

_____

2. How were the soldiers different in the spring?

_____

_____

_____

_____

_____

3. Why were the horses filled with excitement and enthusiasm?

_____

_____

4. Why was the summer such a peaceful time?

_____

_____

5. How did the peaceful life change for Joey and Topthorn?

_____

_____

_____

6. Who was in charge of the cart and horses?

_____

_____

Chapter Thirteen

7. Why was Frederich given the jobs no one else wanted to do?

_____

_____

8. Why were Joey and Topthorn losing weight again and were always tired?

_____

_____

_____

9. How did Frederich try to make the horses' work easier?

_____

_____

_____

10. How did Frederich feel about the war?

_____

_____

11. Where would Frederich rather be then fighting a useless war?

_____

_____

12. Which of the two horses did Frederich favor? Tell why.

_____

_____

13. Why was Frederich willing to risk his life riding on Topthorn's back while the horses pulled the big gun?

_____

_____

_____

Chapter Fourteen

A. Classify the following sentences as "True" or "False" on the line provided.

1. The soldiers prepared themselves to return to fighting in the war one sunny day in the spring. _____

2. The gun troop were resting in the shade of an old apple tree. _____

3. One of the young troopers noticed the quality of Topthorn's breeding. _____

4. Rudi's companion thought horses were wretched creatures with small brains and only knew how to eat and drink. _____

5. Rudi thought horses were noble and regal creatures. _____

6. Many of the troopers looked old and tired to Joey. _____

7. Rudi reminded Joey of Albert and looked like a child dressed up like a soldier. _____

8. Topthorn could not make it back up the steep and rutty hill. _____

9. Topthorn stumbled to his knees at the top of the hill, lay down, looked up at Joey, and died. _____

10. Joey walked away from Topthorn and left him all alone on the ground. _____

11. The veterinary officer was very angry when he examined Topthorn and said, "We should not treat horses like this - we treat machines better. _____

12. The soldiers showed Topthorn respect by cheering and yelling out his name. _____

13. The silence on the hill was broken by the whistle of a shell above the soldiers and the first explosion it made as it landed in the river. _____

14. To escape the shelling, Frederich mounted Joey and galloped up the hill. _____

15. Frederich got his wish and died beside Topthorn. _____

Chapter Fourteen

B. Locate words in the chapter that are antonyms to the following words.

1. peace _____
2. close _____
3. enemy _____
4. weakness _____
5. young _____
6. women _____
7. wrong _____
8. clean _____
9. older _____
10. forgotten _____

11. long _____
12. lightly _____
13. worst _____
14. light _____
15. roughly _____
16. life _____
17. happiness _____
18. dead _____
19. front _____
20. push _____

C. Record how many syllables are heard in each word.

1. intensified _____
2. isolated _____
3. escape _____
4. frantically _____
5. struggled _____
6. abomination _____
7. vigorously _____
8. midday _____
9. fondle _____
10. personality _____
11. surefooted _____
12. damp _____
13. nuzzle _____
14. finality _____
15. grief _____
16. instinctively
17. thoroughbred _____
18. prostrate _____

Chapter Fifteen

Number the sentences that describe Joey's experience in "no man's land" in the correct order.

_____ I ran again for most of the night through ditches, fields with no grass and trees, in and out of craters filled with dirty water.

_____ His strong love and sense of sadness made him stay with Topthorn for as long as he could.

_____ As I was coming out of one crater my foreleg became trapped in a coil of barbed wire.

_____ Quickly I crossed the river and was half way up the wooded hill before I dared to stop and look to see what was after me.

_____ Joey stood by Topthorn and Frederich all day and into the night leaving them once for a drink of water.

_____ Terrified, I left Topthorn's side and ran down the hill towards the river.

_____ Suddenly there was an explosion of white light above my head and the rattle of a machine gun whipped bullets in the ground near me.

_____ As I was nibbling on grass that was close by I heard the terrfying rattle of steel coming closer.

_____ I remembered galloping through farmyards and villages, across rivers, jumping fences, ditches and abandoned trenches until I came to a lush meadow with a clear brook.

_____ Over the top of the hill came a great grey lumbering monster blowing out smoke as it rocked its way down the hill.

Chapter Fifteen

_____ I was so exhausted that I lay down in the grass and slept.

_____ To my surprise, the one monster became several monsters and they were coming after me.

_____ When I kicked wildly to free my leg, the barbs tore my foreleg causing me to limp painfully slow during the night.

_____ When the tanks crossed the river I ran until I could no longer hear their dreadful rattle.

_____ When I awoke I decided to stay where I was because here I had grass to eat and water to drink.

_____ Topthorn and I had charged across it together when we were in the cavalry.

_____ Gunfire was on three sides of me so I headed for the area which was the black horizon.

_____ When the mist cleared, I saw for the first time a wide corridor of mud between two rolls of barbed wire that stretched behind me and in front of me and then I knew I was in what the soldiers call "no man's land."

_____ My injured leg was becoming very stiff and it pained me to even lift it and in time I could not put any weight on it at all.

_____ At dawn, in the autumn mist, I heard voices talking but wanting to be alone and wanting to be away from the noise I slowly limped away.

WAR HORSE
By Michael Morpurgo

Chapter Sixteen

A. Complete each sentence telling what caused the beginning action.

1. Joey knew there were men in the trenches because _____

_____

_____

2. Joey was drawn to both sides of "no man's land" because _____

_____

3. Joey couldn't get near the trenches because _____

_____

4. The German soldier and the Welsh soldier came out of their trenches waving a white flag

because _____

_____

5. The German soldier reminded Joey of Frederich because _____

_____

6. The Welsh soldier regretted coming out of the trench because _____

_____

7. The soldiers were able to communicate because _____

_____

8. The German soldier thinks he should get the horse because _____

_____

9. The men from both sides stopped cheering because_____

_____

10. The Welsh soldier felt the horse needed to get to a veterinary hospital soon because_____

_____

Chapter Sixteen

11. The German soldier suggested they flip a coin for the horse because _____

_____

_____

12. The German soldier handed the rope attached to the horse to the Welsh soldier because

_____

_____

B. Match the words in the word box to their synonyms.

glimpse	savour	beckoning	gap	wafting	tinge
clamber	untidy	cautiously	askew	gash	terrible

1. messy _____
2. cut _____
3. wretched _____
4. space _____
5. climb _____
6. look _____

7. smell _____
8. bit _____
9. waving _____
10. floating _____
11. carefully _____
12. crooked _____

C. Use the correct **homonym** in each sentence.

1. English soldiers wore helmets made of _____ (steal, steel)

2. Joey found it difficult to find his _____ in no man's land. (way, whey, weigh)

3. The German soldier _____ a cap with a red band. (war, wore)

4. The Welsh soldier had the _____ answer. (right, write, rite)

5. There was no way for Joey to get _____ the barbed wire. (through, threw)

6. The German soldier _____ a coin into the air. (through, threw)

WAR HORSE

By Michael Morpurgo

Chapter Seventeen

A. In a story different elements appear in sentences that promote interest for the reader. These sentences may promote emotions, pictures, events, suspense, and mystery.

What does each sentence below promote:

1. visualizes a scene or picture
2. shows emotons, mood in the story
3. describes sounds in a scene
4. describes things happening or taking place in a scene
5. forcasts an event that may take place.
6. displays an element of mystery, surprise, suspense

On the line at the beginning of each sentence record the number of the story element that it reveals to the reader.

_____ 1. The wagon was drawn by two stocky black horses, both well groomed out and immaculate in well-oiled harnesses.

_____ 2. A milling crowd of soldiers surrounded me to cheer me on my way.

_____ 3. My injured leg throbbed terribly as the wagon rocked from side to side on its slow journey away from the battle front.

_____ 4. A reply that sent a sudden shiver of recognition through me.

_____ 5. It confirms my rising hopes and I knew then that I could not be mistaken.

_____ 6. I could just see over the sideboards a wide cobbled courtyard with magnificent stables and a great house with turrets beyond.

_____ 7. My arrival was greeted by a chorus of excited neighing and I raised my head to look.

_____ 8. He's a bright red bay with a black mane and tail. He has a white cross on his forehead and four white socks that are all even to the last inch.

Chapter Seventeen

_____ 9. "I wouldn't have thought it was possible," his friend went on keeping his voice in check. "Not until now that is."

_____ 10. The two men worked tirelessly on me, scraping and brushing and washing.

B. Use the words in the word box to make compound words that match each clue.

stones	yard	board	where	quarters	one
shine	man	stand	side	every	sun
Welsh	any	under	court	cobble	side
under	hind	gate	head	fore	way

1. used on roads and streets   _____

2. an area enclosed by walls   _____

3. a bright light in the summer   _____

4. wood on the sides of a wagon   _____

5. a person who comes from Wales   _____

6. to know something   _____

7. could be many places   _____

8. the bottom of something   _____

9. back end of a horse   _____

10. all, everybody   _____

11. top part of one's face   _____

12. an entrance, entry   _____

Chapter Eighteen

A. Number the sentences in Joey's story in the correct order.

_____   Albert knew there was something wrong because I didn't eat the mash in the bucket.

_____   My front legs were stiff and I stumbled backwards and fell against the brick wall of the stable.

_____   Albert and David begged the Major to help me because he taught them to help injured horses night and day to save them.

_____   My wound was cleaned and stitched up by Major Martin and I was gradually getting better as Albert was with me again.

_____   When I was completely well, Albert led me carefully outside one spring morning for all to see.

_____   Albert ran to get Major Martin who went in the stable alone to examine me.

_____   One morning I was unable to finish eating my mash and every little sound frightened me.

_____   After many long and painful weeks in the sling, I started to feel a looseness in my neck and called out softly to Albert for the first time.

_____   My forelegs would not work and they were stiff and tired and I had great pain all along my spine, creeping into my face and neck.

_____   I backed away in fear as Albert reached out to touch me.

_____   Albert and David agreed to watch over me as much as they could every day, whisper to me, feed me, and provide me with a clean bed of straw.

_____ Major Martin told Albert that I had tetanus and there wasn't much more that he could do for me.

_____ I was placed in a sling attached to the beams in the ceiling of my stall so my feet could not touch the floor.

_____ Days passed slowly and painfully for me but Albert's prescence, his devotion, and his unwavering faith kept me alive.

_____ Major Martin agreed with Sergeant Thunder and said he would help me.

B. A simple sentence contains only one subject and one predicate.
   Example: The school bell rang loudly.
   A compound sentence is one where two or more statements are combined together.
   Example: The school bell ran loudly and the children lined up.
   Write the words "simple" or "compound" after each sentence.

1. I could put little weight on my foot. _____

2. Major Martin cleaned my wound and then he stitched it up. _____

3. I knew from the soft tone of his voice that he was trying to calm me. _____

4. Joey became tense from head to tail. _____

5. I want a sling rigged up in here. _____

6. Albert knew something was wrong when he saw the mash in the bucket. _____

7. His head moved easily and he neighed at me. _____

8. Albert slept in the corner of the stable. _____

9. Joey was taken out of the sling. _____

10. One night I felt a looseness in my throat. _____

WAR HORSE

By Michael Morpurgo

Chapter Nineteen

A. Locate a sentence in the chapter that proves each of the following statements is true.

Record the first six words of the sentence on the line provided.

1. Joey was much stronger and getting better.

_____

2. Joey and Albert always worked together.

_____

3. Joey did not fear the guns at the front line.

_____

4. Albert could only find one fault in Joey.

_____

5. One night Albert received heartbreaking news.

_____

6. Albert had very strong feelings for David.

_____

7. Albert is very determined to get home safely.

_____

8. Albert wants to do three things once he's home.

_____

9. This announced that the end of the war had finally come.

_____

10. Albert was still mourning David's death.

_____

11. Major Martin announced what was to happen to the horses.

_____

12. Major Martin couldn't answer Albert's question about Joey.

_____

WAR HORSE

By Michael Morpurgo

Chapter Nineteen

B. Underline the **subject** and circle the **predicate** in each sentence.

1. Maisie bakes bread like you have never tasted before.

2. Terrible news came from the front one evening.

3. The ominous sound of gunfire was heard again.

4. One day shells crashed near the veterinary wagon.

5. Albert brushed the tears from his eyes.

C. Circle the **conjunction** in each compound sentence.

1. I worked in a team of two, hauling hay and feed or I pulled the dung wagon.

2. Joey was no longer afraid of the guns because Albert was always with him.

3. You're the best listener I've ever known but I never know what you are thinking.

4. There's just you and me left now Joey and I tell you we're going to get home.

5. Major Martin said nothing, but turned on his heel and walked away.

6. Wll the horses be on the ship with the soldiers or will they be coming later.

7. The horses were being sold and left in France.

8. Joey was well yet he could not go home

D. Underline the **root word** in each word below and write it on the line provided..

1. illness _____

2. whistling _____

3. reminder _____

4. tastiest _____

5. listener _____

6. unexpectedly _____

7. disguising _____

8. gritted _____

9. celebration _____

10. almost _____

WAR HORSE

By Michael Morpurgo

Chapter Twenty

A. Complete the following activities.

1. List some words and phrases that describe the mood in the yard that day.

_____

_____

_____

2. What had the soldiers been conspiring?

_____

_____

3. Who was in charge of the bidding?

_____

_____

4. Why was Joey happy to listen to Albert that night?

_____

_____

5. Who were the last two bidders in the auction?

_____

_____

6. Why could Joey barely look at the second bidder?

_____

_____

7. Why did Albert get so upset when Sergeant Thunder shook his head and looked down during the bidding?

_____

_____

8. Whose voice upset the bidding and prevented Monsieur Cirac from getting Joey? Tell why?

_____

_____

WAR HORSE

By Michael Morpurgo

Chapter Twenty-One

A. Answer the following questions with sentences.

1. Tell why everyone was relieved when Emilie's grandfather had bought Joey?

_____

_____

2. Why was Albert not satisfied with who had purchased Joey?

_____

_____

3. List the things Albert learned about Emilie from her grandfather.

_____

_____

_____

_____

_____

4. What promise did Emilie want her grandfather to make and keep?

_____

_____

5. What was the proposition Emilie's grandfather made to Albert?

_____

_____

_____

6. What else did Emile's grandfather want him to do?

_____

_____

_____

7. Why did Emilie's grandfather want Albert to talk about his Emilie?

_____

_____

_____

8. How do you think Emilie's grandfather felt letting Joey go with Albert?

_____

_____

WAR HORSE

By Michael Morpurgo

Chapter Twenty-One

9. List the ways this story has a happy ending.

_____
_____
_____
_____
_____
_____
_____
_____
_____
_____
_____

10. Why do you think there was a mutual jealousy between Maisie and Joey?

_____
_____

11. Ilustrate a scene that you might see in the last chapter.

WAR HORSE

By Michael Morpurgo

Answer Key

Author Notes: Page 14

1. He describes an old oil painting of a horse that hangs in the Village Hall.
2. The horse is a splendid red bay with a white cross on his forehead and has four identical white socks.
3. The horse is called Joey and the painting was done by Captain James Nicholls.
4. It was painted in the autumn of 1914.
5. World War I had begun in Europe.
6. Most of the people who knew Joey have died.
7. The author wants people to remember Joey, the war, and those who died in it.
8. Student Response will vary.

Chapter One: Page 15 to 16

A. 1. Joey, the horse, is telling the story.
   2. The young horse was almost six months old and a gangling, leggy colt
   3. His mother was sold and taken away from him and he would never see her again.
   4. He was very young and no one wanted to pay good money for a spindley-looking, half-thoroughbred colt.
   5. Albert's father bought him for three guineas to annoy a man he did not like and he was too drunk to know what he was doing.
   6. He was supposed to buy a calf to suckle old Celandine.
   7. Albert's father treated the young horse in a very cruel manner. Only one man would ever be his master.
   8. He was dragged on a short rope attached to the tailboard of a farm cart. He was soaking wet from exhaustion and the halter had rubbed his face raw.
   9. Zoey nickered at him in kindness and sympathy that calmed Joey and soothed his spirit.
  10. Albert rubbed Joey down until he was dry. He talked and touched him gently. He put salted water on the sores on his face and body and fed him sweet hay and water.
  11. Albert named him Joey because it rhymed with Zoey's name.
  12. Student Response will vary.

B. 1. gangling, gently, glimpse, gritted, groom
   2. halter, harsh, hauled, hubbub, huddled
   3. screamed, stamina, stranded, strength, struggle
   4. tailboard, thirteen, thoroughbred, through, touch
   5. lacked, leant, life, lone, lunge
   6. eating, echoing, enough, excited, exhaustion
   7. mane, managed, memories, market, master
   8. barney, beaming, bidding, brought, bucket

WAR HORSE

By Michael Morpurgo

Chapter Two Page: 17 to 18   Part A

1. He trained Joey and taught him to come with a special whistle.
2. Joey found it lonely in the winter and found the summer days bearable because he could hear Zoey working in the fields and would call out to her.
3. Joey never trusted him and never let him come too close.
4. Albert's father came to try some collars on Joey because people in the village said he couldn't have him plowing in a week.
5. Joey couldn't get away so he kicked Albert's father with his back feet.
6. Albert is to have Joey trained to plow straight as an arrow in a week so his father can win his bet.
7. Albert's father was so angry with Joey for kicking him, he would have shot him.
8. Joey would be sold.
9. Albert spoke harshly and sharply and used a whip.
10. His father won his bet and said he would forget all about the incident.
11. War was declared at eleven o'clock in the morning against the Germans.
12. Albert's mother was upset and his father was determined the war would be over in a few months.

B. 1. pretext 2. affection 3. bearable 4. recesses 5. companion 6. precaution 7. encounter
   8. prowess 9. molly-coddled 10. cruel 11. survive 12. imitated

Chapter Three   Page: 19 to 20   Part A

1. Albert had taken over most of the horsework on the farm.
2. Albert's mother and father had arguments as well as Albert and his mother.
3. he bought the farm for him to own when he grows up.
4. he's worried about paying the mortgage on the farm, the war, and prices falling back.
5. his father was always complaining about work not being done, him riding Joey in the evenings, and when he does his bell-ringing.
6. horses cost too much to feed and he regrets buying Joey.
7. they scarcely spoke to each other any more.
8. he didn't want to upset his mother.
9. he always came in for Zoey to take him into the hills to check the sheep.
10. he talked to him sweetly and had a bucket of sweet-smelling oats.
11. he wanted to put a halter over his head.
12. he spoke softly, stroked his neck and told him he needs the money.

B. 1. reason 2. complain 3. declare 4. hard 5. ditch 6. angry 7. worry 8. pig 9. tight
   10. usual 11. arbitrate 12. change

C. 1. inquisitiveness 2. tension 3. foreboding 4. acute 5. arbitrator 6. vehemently 7. copse
   8. suspicious 9. arbitrating 10. reasonable

WAR HORSE
By Michael Morpurgo

Chapter Four   Page: 21 to 22   Part A
1. All the while I noticed Page 27
2. Excited as I was, I Page 28
3. "It's because I need the money." Page 29
4. "I'd thought you'd be exaggerating." Page 29
5. "You're right, farmer, he'd make   Page 29
6. "Forty pounds you'll pay me, Captain."   Page 29
7. "Well," said the officer, as long" Page 30
8. "I can't be long, sir," Page 30
9. Joey passed the vet's examination Page 31
10. "You'll look after him sir?"   Page 31
11. "I'll find you again, you old silly, Page 34
12. "I promise," said Captain Nicholls   Page 34

B. 1. adjective 2. adverb 3. noun 4. verb 5. verb 6. adjectives 7. adjective 8. noun
C. 1. short 2. quietly 3. slowly 4. gently 5. finest 6. deep 7. straight 8. openly
   9. whispered 10. buying

Chapter Five   Page: 23 to 24   Part A
1. Student Response may vary but should have similar points.
   Life as a Farm Horse:
   • loved his long rides with Albert
   • the heat and the flies didn't bother him
   • loved ploughing the fields with Zoey
   • enjoyed the bond of trust and devotion between Albert and himself
   Life as a Cavalry Horse:
   • did not like the strict disciplines of the riding school
   • found it was hot and hard during manoeuvres
   • tedious hours were spent circling the school
   • had to wear a large bit that hurt his mouth
   • did not like his trainer as he rode him hard and used his spurs and whip alot
2. Captain Nicholls came every evening to talk to Joey and to sketch a picture of him.
3. Captain Nicholls plans to send the picture to Albert so he will know he is keeping his promise.
4. Captain Nicholls feels the war is going to be a nasty one and hopes it is over before Albert is old enough to join.
5. Captain Nicholls wants Joey trained in a gentler way and fed better to improve his condition because he wants Joey to be the best looking horse in the squadron.
6. Yes he did. He used his spurs less and gave Joey more freedom. He fed Joey better and gave him unending care and attention.
7. He found Captain Nicholls weighed heavier on his back. It was hot and the flies bothered him. The cavalry charge filled him with great excitement.
9. Joey met Topthorn a huge, shiny, black stallion who ran as fast as him.

OTM-14287 ISBN: 9781770787995

WAR HORSE

By Michael Morpurgo

9. The soldiers and the horses left for France in a large ship.
B. 1. devotion 2. revelled 3. sabre 4. trepidation 5. rubbish 6. tedious 7. charge
   8. transformation

Chapter Six   Page 25 to 26   Part A.
1. • Soldiers were happy and optimistic.
    • They did not have a care in the world.
    • They felt they were having a big picnic.
    • The soldiers laughed and joked.
    • The horses were very upset and afraid and kicked their stalls trying to break them.
    • The horses did not like the pitching and rolling of the ship.
2. The soldiers were silent and sombre when they saw all the wounded men and the horses calmed down once they were on solid ground.
3. They realized the kind of war they were going to and how unprepared they were to fight.
4. • Stopped every hour for a few minutes rest.
    • Often walked beside them.
    • Brought them buckets of sweet water from nearby streams.
    • Fed them well and let them graze.
5. He heard the thunder of the big guns getting louder and at night he saw orange flashes from one end of the horizon to the other.
6. Topthorn gave him courage and always walked beside him.
7. Joey lost Captain Nicholls and was alone at the head of the squadron and ran right through the enemy lines.
8. Joey kept on running because he was so terrified and wanted to get away.
9. Topthorn rode up beside him and Captain Stewart grabbed his reins.
10. Captain Stewart told Joey Captain Nicholls would have been very proud of the way he led the charge without him.
11. Joey feels sad about Captain Nicholls and longs for home.
B. 1. veil of sadness; covering of unhappiness
    2. a feeling of joyfuness and waiting
    3. floating with enthusiasm
    4. very weary and filled with fear
    5. horses were tied together
    6. gradual roaring, getting louder
    7. made me very weak

Chapter Seven   Page 27 to 28
A. Sequential ordering of Sentences: 4, 9, 6, 11, 1, 5, 12, 2, 7, 3, 8, 10
B. Student Drawings will vary.
C. 1. horseman 2. blacksmith 3. horselines 4. onset 5. overrun 6. deadlock 7. dugout 8. alongside
    9. nosebag 10 greatcoat 11. forelock 12. motorcycle

WAR HORSE

By Michael Morpurgo

Chapter Eight   Page: 29 to 30

A. 1. False   2. True   3. True   4. False   5. False   6. True   7. False   8. True   9. True   10. False

B. jingle of the harness; snorting of the horses; shells falling; machine-guns firing; screams of the men and horses; shells whined and roared; explosions; horses galloping; rifle-fire

C. He hoped they would finally see that you can't send horses into wire and machine-guns.

D. 1. nouns   2. verbs   3. adverb   4. adjective   5. phrases   6. clause

Chapter Nine   Page 31 to 32

A. Sequential Order of Sentences: 5, 11, 4, 1, 7, 8, 10, 2, 6, 3, 9

B. 1. when   2. what   3. where   4. what   5. when   6. where   7. why   8. how   9. who   10. what   11. how   12. where   13. where   14. how   15. what   16. where   17. when   18. what   19. when   20. where   21. where   22. when   23. what   24. where

C. 1. nouns   2. adjective   3. adverb phrase   4. adjectives   5. verbs   6. adverb

Chapter Ten   Page 33 to 34   Part A

1. • Marching men cheered them as they passed by.
   • One soldier threw his arm around Joey's head and kissed him and gave him a German medal called the Iron Cross.
   • Waiting wounded outside a hospital cheered and clapped for them.
   • Able wounded soldiers visited them at the stable to compliment them and to give them treats.

2. • Emilie and her grandfather waiting by the stable door every evening.
   • The care that they had received from them.
   • Emilie's chats with the horses.
   • Emilie taking them to a field to graze.
   • Emilie making a fringe to protect their eyes from flies.
   • Emilie standing on the wall waving to them when they left.

3. Children speak softly and their size does not threathen them.

4. • Greeted them every evening by the stable door.
   • Fed them, rubbed them down, cleaned and cared for their feet.
   • Got up at dawn to feed them before they went to work.
   • Spent as much time with them as she could.
   • Stood on the wall and waved until they were out of sight.

5. Emily was not there to greet them and her grandfather fed them quickly and did not say a word.

6. They sensed something was wrong.

7. He told them that Emilie had pneumonia and the doctor has done all he can for her and now its up to God to make her well.

8. He fears she will die and there will be no one left in his family.

9. He asks them to pray for Emilie as she prays for them every day.

10. The snow hid the ruts and shell holes and the piled up snow and sinking mud made it difficult to pull the cart.

11. It was Christmas Day

WAR HORSE

By Michael Morpurgo

12. Emilie's grandfather told them she awakened at lunchtime and wanted to get up to feed the horses.
13. The only way she would stay in bed was if the doctor promised to give the horses extra rations during the cold weather.
14. The grandfather's Christmas present was Emilie getting better and the horses got extra mash and hay.

Chapter Eleven   Page 35 to 36   Part A
1. there were fewer wounded soldiers and they were needed less to pull the ambulance cart.
2. he was much taller and broader than Joey.
3. the doctor wanted to tell Emilie and her grandfather the horses could stay longer on the farm.
4. they have to keep on working the farm to grow their own food so they can eat.
5. their faces were severe and hard and they had an urgency in their eyes.
6. he went over to stroke the horses and spoke kindly to Emilie.
7. they were to0 tired to reply.
8. he had eyes like a wasp and you can't trust a wasp.
9. he was unable to stop the soldiers.
10. she was to be proud and strong like her brother.
B. 1. thunder 2. fewer 3. dark 4. gently 5. difficult 6. sad 7. long 8. hard 9. soft 10. laugh 11. early   12. before
C. 1. weak 2. heard 3. great 4. team 5. peace 6. mane 7. reins 8. pare
D. Sentences will vary

Chapter Twelve   Page 37 to 38   Part A
1. • Guns were lined up only a few yards apart for miles.
   • When the guns were being used the earth shook beneath them.
   • The lines of the wounded soldiers went on forever.
   • The countryside was a wasteland for miles.
2. • They were not stabled at night.
   • The noise was scary and the battlefield smelled.
   • The horses were often whipped by the men to get the guns where they should be.
   • Food was scarce and the horses had little to eat.
   • The horses began to lose weight and their conditions worsened.
   • They worked longer and harder hours.
   • The horses were always sore, cold, tired, and covered with mud.
3. a) Topthorn and Heinie b) Joey c) Coco d) two golden Haflingers e) Coco f) Heinie g) Coco h) two golden Halkingers i) Heinie j) Joey k) Coco l) Topthorn m) Heinie n) Joey
B. 1. (4) 2. (2) 3. (5) 4. (2) 5. (1) 6. (6) 7. (1) 8. (2) 9. (5) 10. (2) 11. (5) 12. (3) 13. (4) 14. (4) 15. (3)

Chapter Thirteen   Page 39 to 40   Part A
1. They had both survived. Topthorn was weak and still had a cough. Their bodies filled out from eating grass. The ground was hard and easier to walk on. They lost their raggedy winter coats. Sores

WAR HORSE
By Michael Morpurgo

disappeared from their legs. They had full bellies.

2. Their uniforms were cleaner. They were happier and treated the horses better. They talked about the war coming to an end and going home to their families.

3. Their new-found health and the optimism of the singing, whistling soldiers made them feel good.

4. There were no battles nearby so the guns did not have to be moved.

5. Joey and Topthorn were selected to pull the ammunition cart from the nearby railhead to the artillery lines.

6. A kind old soldier that everyone called mad old Frederich because he talked and laughed to himself all the time.

7. He was always obliging and everyone knew it.

8. The loaded carts were too heavy for them to pull easily.

9. They stopped often for rests and drinks of water. Frederich would walk beside the wagon up hills. He fed them better than the other horses.

10. Frederich hated the war because men were fighting and killing each other and they didn't know why.

11. Frederich would rather be in his butcher shop and with his family.

12. Frederich preferred Topthorn as they seemed to know how each other felt.

13. If he has to die in this war he would rather die beside Topthorn.

Chapter Fourteen   Page 41 to 42   Part A
1. False 2. False 3. True 4. True 5. True 6. False 7. True 8. False 9. True 10. False
11. True 12. False 13. True 14. False 15. True
B. 1. war 2. open 3. friend 4. strength 5. old 6. men 7. right 8. filthy 9. younger 10. remembered
   11. short 12. heavily 13. best 13. heavy 14. heavy 15. gently 16. death 17. sadness
   18. alive 19. behind 20. pull
C. 1. (4) 2. (4) 3. (2) 4. (4) 5. (2) 6. (5) 7. (4) 8. (2) 9. (2) 10. (5) 11. (3) 12. (1) 13. (2)
   14. (4) 15. (1) 16. (4) 17. (3) 18. (2)

Chapter Fifteen   Page 43 to 44
Sequence Order of Sentences: 13, 2, 14, 6, 1, 5, 12, 3, 9, 4, 10, 7, 15, 8, 11, 20, 16, 19, 17, 18

Chapter Sixteen Page 45 to 46   Part A
1. he heard laughter and someone barking orders and saw the occasional steel helmet.
2. he could smell food cooking.
3. there was a barrier of loosely coiled barbed wire.
4. they both wanted to help the horse.
5. he had grey hair, spoke gently, and wore an untidy uniform.
6. he couldn't speak German and doesn't know how to solve the problem of the horse.
7. the German soldier could speak a little English.
8. he was out of the trench first.
9. they wanted to hear what the men were discussing.
10. the horse's leg may become infected.
11. no one will lose any pride and everyone will be happy.

WAR HORSE

By Michael Morpurgo

12. he picked the right side of the coin.

B. 1. untidy 2. gash 3. terrible 4. gap 5. clamber 6. glimpse 7. savour 8. tinge 9. beckoning
10. wafting 11. cautiously 12. askew

C. 1. steel 2. way 3. wore 4. right 5. through 6. threw

Chapter Seventeen   Page 47 to 48

A. 1. (1) 2. (3) 3. (2) 4. (6) 5. (2) 6. (1) 7. (3) 8. (1) 9. (6) 10. (5)

B. 1. cobblestone 2. courtyard 3. sunshine 4. sideboard 5. Welshman 6. understand 7. anywhere
   8. underside 9. hindquarters 10. everyone 11. forehead 12. gateway

Chapter Eighteen   Page 49 to 50

A. Sequential Order of Sentences: 4, 6, 9, 1, 15, 7, 2, 14, 3, 5, 12, 8, 11, 13, 10

B. 1. Simple 2. Compound 3. Compound 4. Simple 5. Simple 6. Compound 7. Compound
   8. Simple 9. Simple 10. Simple

Chapter Nineteen Page 51 to 52   Part A

   1. My convalescence was almost over now.
   2. Sergeant Thunder had detailed Albert to
   3. But Albert was always with me and
   4. That's the only thing I've got against
   5. Then one evening there was terrible
   6. Like a brother he was to
   7. There's just you and me left now
   8. I'm going to ring that tenor
   9. The bell in the clock tower over
10. Since David's death Albert had not
11. The horses will be staying in
12. Major Martin said nothing, but

B. 1. Subject: Maisie   Predicate: bakes
   2. Subject: news   Predicate: came
   3. Subject: sound   Predicate: heard
   4. Subject: shells   Predicate: crashed
   5. Subject: Albert   Predicate: brushed

C. 1. or 2. because 3. but 4. and 5. but 6. or 7. and 8. yet

D. 1. ill 2. whistle 3. mind 4. tasty 5. listen 6. expect 7. disguise 8. grit 9. celebrate 10. most

Chapter Twenty   Page: 53 to 54   Part A

   1. conspiracy, whispering, huddled together, anxiety, impatient soldiers
   2. They were collecting money to buy Joey for Albert during the auction.
   3. Sergeant Thunder was going to do the bidding.
   4. Joey had not heard Albert talk to him like that since David had been reported killed.
   5. Sergeant Thunder and a thing wiry man with weasel-like eyes.
   6. He had eyes like a weasel and a smile that was full of greed and evil.

OTM-14287 ISBN: 9781770787995

WAR HORSE

By Michael Morpurgo

7. Sergeant Thunder didn't have any more money to outbid Monsieur Cirac of Cambria.

8. It was Emilie's grandfather's voice that upset the bidding. He was willing to pay 100 English pounds for Joey.

Chapter Twenty-One   Page: 54 to 55   Part A.

1. Many of the horses had gone to butchers whereas Joey was safe with the old farmer man

2. He still wants Joey and thinks the old farmer is as mad as a hatter because he calls Joey, Emilie's horse.

3. Emilie had loved and cared for Joey and Topthorn. They were her family. Her parents had been killed during the beginning of the war. Her grandfather was her only living relative. When the horses were taken away by the Germans she lost the will to live and died.

4. He promised her he would find the horses somehow to look after them.

5. Albert could buy Joey from him for one English penny and a promise to love and care for the horse until the end of his days.

6. He wanted Albert to tell about his Emilie and how she had cared for and loved Joey and the big black horse too.

7. He wanted Emilie to live on in the hearts of people because when he dies no one will remember his Emilie as she was. There is no family left.

8. He was at peace with himself and Emilie would have been very happy.

9. • Joey and Albert ride into town welcomed by a band playing and church bells ringing.
   • Albert married Maisie Cobbledick.
   • Joey was back working with Zoey.
   • Albert's father dotted on Joey.
   • Joey took over running his father's farm and went back to ringing the tenor bell.

10. They both want Albert's love and attention.

11. Chapter Scenes will vary.

www.ingramcontent.com/pod-product-compliance
Lightning Source LLC
Chambersburg PA
CBHW081325020726
47506CB00005B/1184